POEMS F
7 YEAR O

Susie Gibbs has worked in the world of children's poetry for ten years. Her eight nephews and nieces were invaluable testing grounds for *Poems for 7 Year Olds*, and she very much hopes that they and their friends will enjoy this selection. Having recently taken her narrowboat, *Hesperus II*, to Wigan Pier and back, Susie now lives aboard it on the River Thames with no pets but plenty of wildlife.

Wendy Smith has been writing and illustrating children's books for 25 years. A graduate of the RCA, she currently teaches at the University of Brighton. She has many interests including poetry, and much enjoys living by the Regent's Canal in Camden Town.

Also available from Macmillan Children's Books

POEMS FOR 8 YEAR OLDS
Chosen by Susie Gibbs

POEMS FOR 9 YEAR OLDS
Chosen by Susie Gibbs

GOLDEN APPLES
Chosen by Fiona Waters

READ ME 1
A Poem for Every Day of the Year
Chosen by Gaby Morgan

UNZIP YOUR LIPS!
100 poems to read out loud
Chosen by Paul Cookson

ANOTHER DAY ON YOUR FOOT AND I WOULD HAVE DIED!
Poems by John Agard, Wendy Cope, Roger McGough, Adrian Mitchell and Brian Patten

POEMS FOR 7 YEAR OLDS

CHOSEN BY

Susie Gibbs

ILLUSTRATED BY

Wendy Smith

MACMILLAN CHILDREN'S BOOKS

Dedicated with love to all my nephews and nieces:
George Henry Cormick, Nicholas John, Mustafa Noah, Lütfiye, Patrick Charles, Hatice Sara, Ayse Filiz and Zenda Amy Lily Sunshine.

First published 1999
by Macmillan Children's Books
a division of Macmillan Publishers Ltd
25 Eccleston Place, London SW1W 9NF
Basingstoke and Oxford
www.macmillan.co.uk

Associated companies throughout the world

ISBN 0 330 37182 7

1 3 5 7 9 8 6 4 2

A CIP catalogue record for this book is available from the British Library.

Printed by Mackays of Chatham plc, Chatham, Kent.

Contents

Dick's Dog

Dick had a dog
The dog dug
The dog dug deep
How deep did Dick's dog dig?

Dick had a duck
The duck dived
The duck dived deep
How deep did Dick's duck dive?

Dick's duck dived as deep as Dick's dog dug.

Trevor Millum

Magic Cat

My mum whilst walking through the door
spilt some magic on the floor.
Blobs of this
and splots of that
but most of it upon the cat.

Our cat turned magic, straight away
and in the garden went to play
where it grew two massive wings
and flew around in fancy rings.
'Oh look!' cried Mother, pointing high,
'I didn't know our cat could fly.'
Then with a dash of Tibby's tail
she turned my mum into a snail!

So now she lives beneath a stone
and dusts around a different home.
And I'm an ant
and Dad's a mouse
and Tibby's living in our house.

Peter Dixon

Town Dog

I'm a town dog.
Usually I walk on a lead with my mistress;
I let children pat my head,
And politely use the gutter.
But sometimes,
Sometimes,
When it's
late
and dark
and shiny
and shadowy
and everyone is in bed,
I let myself out of the house
(Turning the key in my teeth),
Wearing my wolf's head
And my extra sharp fangs,
And I run and run
And have thrilling moonlit adventures.

And in the morning she says
'Tut-tut,
Who left the door open?'
and
'Tut-tut.
Look at that lazy dog. He needs more exercise!'

David Orme

Barry and Beryl the Bubble Gum Blowers

Barry and Beryl the bubble gum blowers
blew bubble gum bubbles as big as balloons.
All shapes and sizes, zebras and zeppelins,
swordfish and sealions, sharks and baboons,
babies and buckets, bottles and biplanes,
buffaloes, bees, trombones and bassoons.
Barry and Beryl the bubble gum blowers
blew bubble gum bubbles as big as balloons.

Barry and Beryl the bubble gum blowers
blew bubble gum bubbles all over the place.
Big ones in bed, on backseats of buses,
blowing their bubbles in baths with bad taste,
they blew and they bubbled from breakfast till
bedtime
the biggest gum bubble that history traced.
One last big breath . . . and the bubble exploded
bursting and blasting their heads into space.
Yes Barry and Beryl the bubble gum blowers
blew bubbles that blasted their heads into space.

Paul Cookson

Mother Alligator's Advice to Her Children

Don't eat too much sweet
You'll spoil your lovely teeth.

Don't touch jelly or treacle
Stick to eating people.

John Agard

The Fairies

Up the airy mountain,
Down the rushy glen,
We daren't go a-hunting
For fear of little men;
Wee folk, good folk,
Trooping all together;
Green jacket, red cap,
And white owl's feather!

Down along the rocky shore
Some make their home,
They live on crispy pancakes
Of yellow tide-foam;
Some in the reeds
Of the black mountain lake,
With frogs for their watch-dogs,
All night awake.

High on the hill-top
The old King sits;
He is now so old and grey
He's nigh lost his wits.
With a bridge of white mist
Columbkill he crosses,
On his stately journeys
From Slieveleague to Rosses;
Or going up with music
On cold starry nights
To sup with the Queen
Of the gay Northern Lights.

They stole little Bridget
For seven years long;
When she came down again
Her friends were all gone.
They took her lightly back,
Between the night and morrow,
They thought that she was fast asleep,
But she was dead with sorrow.
They have kept her ever since
Deep within the lake,
On a bed of flag-leaves,

Watching till she wake.
By the craggy hill-side,
Through the mosses bare,
They have planted thorn-trees
For pleasure here and there.
If any man so daring
As dig them up in spite,
He shall find their sharpest thorns
In his bed at night.

Up the airy mountain,
Down the rushy glen,
We daren't go a-hunting
For fear of little men;
Wee folk, good folk,
Trooping all together;
Green jacket, red cap,
And white owl's feather!

William Allingham

My Baby Brother

My baby brother is a killer
He pulls my hair and throws me down
on the floor and spits in my face and
squeezes my nose and takes off my
glasses and then tries them on and
throws them away and he jumps on
my stomach and he bites my toes and
he counts my fingers and my mother
says, 'Ian get off the floor.'

Ian Aitken

Bedtime

When I go upstairs to bed,
I usually give a loud cough.
This is to scare The Monster off.

When I come to my room,
I usually slam the door right back.
This is to squash The Man in Black
Who sometimes hides there.

Nor do I walk to the bed,
But usually run and jump instead.
This is to stop The Hand –
Which is under there all right –
From grabbing my ankles.

Allan Ahlberg

The Old Person of Fratton

There was an old person of Fratton
Who would go to church with his hat on.
  'If I wake up,' he said,
  'With my hat on my head,
I shall know that it hasn't been sat on.'

Anon

Peculiar

I once knew a boy who was odd as could be:
He liked to eat cauliflower and broccoli
And spinach and turnips and rhubarb pies
And he didn't like hamburgers or French-fries.

Eve Merriam

Humpty Dumpty's Recitation

In winter, when the fields are white,
I sing this song for your delight –

In spring, when woods are getting green,
I'll try and tell you what I mean.

In summer, when the days are long,
Perhaps you'll understand the song.

In autumn, when the leaves are brown,
Take pen and ink and write it down.

I sent a message to the fish:
I told them 'This is what I wish.'

The little fishes of the sea
They sent an answer back to me.

The little fishes' answer was
'We cannot do it, Sir, because – '

I sent to them again to say
'It will be better to obey.'

The fishes answered with a grin,
'Why, what a temper you are in!'

I told them once, I told them twice:
They would not listen to advice.

I took a kettle large and new,
Fit for the deed I had to do.

My heart went hop, my heart went thump;
I filled the kettle at the pump.

Then someone came to me and said
'The little fishes are in bed.'

I said to him, I said it plain,
'Then you must wake them up again.'

I said it loud and very clear;
I went and shouted in his ear.

But he was very stiff and proud;
He said 'You needn't shout so loud!'

And he was very proud and stiff;
He said 'I'll go and wake them, if –'

I took a corkscrew from the shelf:
I went to wake them up myself.

And when I found the door was locked,
I pulled and pushed and kicked and knocked.

And when I found the door was shut,
I tried to turn the handle, but –

Lewis Carroll

This Old Man

This old man
He played one
He played nicknack on my bum.
Nicknack paddywhack
Give a dog a bone
This old man came rolling home.

This old man
He played two
He played nicknack on my shoe.
Nicknack paddywhack
Give a dog a bone
This old man came rolling home.

This old man
He played three
He played nicknack on my knee.
Nicknack paddywhack
Give a dog a bone
This old man came rolling home.

1
2
3
4
5
6
7
8
9
10

This old man
He played four
He played nicknack on my door.
Nicknack paddywhack
Give a dog a bone
This old man came rolling home.

This old man
He played five
He played nicknack on my hide.
Nicknack paddywhack
Give a dog a bone
This old man came rolling home.

This old man
He played six
He played nicknack on my knicks.
Nicknack paddywhack
Give a dog a bone
This old man came rolling home.

This old man
He played seven
He played nicknack up to Heaven.
Nicknack paddywhack
Give a dog a bone
This old man came rolling home.

This old man
He played eight
He played nicknack on my plate.
Nicknack paddywhack
Give a dog a bone
This old man came rolling home.

This old man
He played nine
He played nicknack on my spine.
Nicknack paddywhack
Give a dog a bone
This old man came rolling home.

This old man
He played ten
He played nicknack on my pen.
Nicknack paddywhack
Give a dog a bone
This old man came rolling home.

Anon

The New Year

I am the little New Year, ho, ho!
Here I come tripping it over the snow.
Shaking my bells with a merry din –
So open your doors and let me in!

Presents I bring for each and all –
Big folks, little folks, short and tall;
Each one from me a treasure may win –
So open your doors and let me in!

Some shall have silver and some shall have gold,
Some shall have new clothes and some shall
  have old;
Some shall have brass and some shall have tin –
So open your doors and let me in!

Some shall have water and some shall have milk,
Some shall have satin and some shall have silk!
But each from me a present may win –
So open your doors and let me in!

Anon

Fuzzy-Wuzzy

Fuzzy-Wuzzy was a bear
Fuzzy-Wuzzy had no hair
So Fuzzy-Wuzzy wasn't fuzzy, wuzzy?

Anon

'Quack!' Said the Billy-Goat

'Quack!' said the billy-goat.
'Oink!' said the hen.
'Miaow!' said the little chick
Running in the pen.

'Hobble-gobble!' said the dog.
'Cluck!' said the sow.
'Tu-whit tu-whoo!' the donkey said.
'Baa!' said the cow.

'Hee-haw!' the turkey cried.
The duck began to moo.
All at once the sheep went,
'Cock-a-doodle-doo!'

The owl coughed and cleared his throat
And he began to bleat.
'Bow-wow!' said the cock
Swimming in the leat.

'Cheep-cheep!' said the cat
As she began to fly.
'Farmer's been and laid an egg –
That's the reason why.'

Charles Causley

The Months

January brings the snow,
Makes our feet and fingers glow.

February brings the rain,
Thaws the frozen lake again.

March brings breezes loud and shrill,
Stirs the dancing daffodil.

April brings the primrose sweet,
Scatters daisies at our feet.

May brings flocks of pretty lambs,
Skipping by their fleecy dams.

June brings tulips, lilies, roses,
Fills the children's hands with posies.

Hot July brings cooling showers,
Apricots and gillyflowers.

August brings the sheaves of corn,
Then the harvest home is borne.

Warm September brings the fruit,
Sportsmen then begin to shoot.

Fresh October brings the pheasant,
Then to gather nuts is pleasant.

Dull November brings the blast,
Then the leaves are whirling fast.

Chill December brings the sleet,
Blazing fire, and Christmas treat.

Sara Coleridge

No Hickory No Dickory No Dock

Wasn't me
Wasn't me
said the little mouse
I didn't run up no clock

You could hickory me
You could dickory me
or lock me in a dock

I still say
I didn't run up no clock

Was me who ran under your bed
Was me who bit into your bread
Was me who nibbled your cheese

But please please,
I didn't run up no clock
no hickory
no dickory
no dock.

John Agard

Christmas Eve Trip

If you hear a creak at Christmas
in the middle of the night,
it'll just be Santa searching
To find your toilet light.

For after flying round the world
and one sherry too many,
Santa will always need to stop
and spend a little penny.

Andrew Collett

My Team's Not Scoring

It's raining it's pouring
And my team's not scoring.
So boring no scoring
Their goalkeeper's yawning.
He could rest his head
In the back of the net
And still, we'd have no
Chance of scoring.

It's raining it's pouring
Now I'm the one that's yawning.
No scoring so boring
No chance of EVER scoring.
See me rest my head
On the shoulder of Ted
Who doesn't object
To my snoring.

Not raining nor pouring
Now the crowd are roaring.
Not boring not boring
As I feel myself soaring,
To deflect with my head
The centre from Ted
Now I'm the hero
For scoring.

Not raining nor pouring
I hear the fans applauding.
Not boring I'm scoring
Their faith I am . . . . . . what? eh? oh!
It's raining it's pouring
And I've just missed us
SCORING!

Ian Blackman

Mum for a Day

Mum's ill in bed today
so I said I'd do the housework and look after
things.
She told me it was really hard
but I said it'd be dead easy.
So . . .

I hoovered up the sink.

I dusted the cat.

I cooked my dad's shoes.

I washed up the carpet.

I fed all the ornaments and pictures.

Polished the steak and kidney pudding and
chips.

Ironed all the letters and parcels.

Posted all the shirts and knickers.

Last of all . . .
I hung the budgie out on the washing line to
  dry.

It took me all day
but I got everything finished
and I was really tired.

I'm really glad Mum isn't ill every day
and do you know what?

So is the budgie.

Paul Cookson

Muuuuuuummmmmm

Can we have a kitten
Can we have a dog
Can we call her Frisky
Can we call him Bob?
I can take him out each day
I can brush his fur
I will buy the dog meat
And milk to make her purrrr
Mum!!!

Oh . . . no . . .
Well –

Can we have a donkey
or can we have a horse
a monkey or a parrot
hamster or a snake?
Can we have a guinea pig
a peahen
or a stoat,
lama or a budgie
a rabbit or a goat?

Can we have a crocodile
gibbon or an owl,
all the zoos are closing
there's lots and lots around . . .
A penguin would be really good
keep it in the bath
hyena in the garden
  to make the milkman laugh.

No, WE DON'T WANT stick insects
and goldfish aren't much fun . . .

Oh, can we have a puppy . . .
  Mum
    Mum
      Muuuuuuummmmmmmm.

Peter Dixon

Twiddling Your Thumbs

When you've finished all your writing
And you've got stuck with your sums
And you need to see your teacher
But your turn never comes,
You may have time to practise this –
Twiddling your thumbs.

Round and round and round they go,
Forwards, backwards, fast or slow,
Then, if you should get the chance,
Make them do a little dance.

When you've eaten up your dinner,
Including all the crumbs,
And you're waiting for permission
To go out with your chums,
Here's a way to pass the time –
Twiddling your thumbs.

Round and round and round they go,
Forwards, backwards, fast or slow,
Then, if you should get the chance,
Make them do a little dance.

If you have to go out visiting
With aunts and dads and mums
And it's boring being with grown-ups
All sitting on their bums,
Don't scream and bite the carpet –
Try twiddling your thumbs.

Round and round and round they go,
Forwards, backwards, fast or slow,
Then, if you should get the chance,
Make them do a little dance.

Wendy Cope

Bramble Talk

A caterpillar on a leaf
Said sadly to another:
'So many pretty butterflies . . .

I wonder which one's Mother.'

Richard Edwards

I Know an Old Lady Who Swallowed a Fly

(extract)

I know an old lady who swallowed a cow,
Don't ask how she swallowed a cow.
She swallowed the cow to catch the goat,
Popped open her throat and swallowed a goat.
She swallowed the goat to catch the dog,
Oh, what a hog to swallow a dog!
She swallowed the dog to catch the cat.
Think of that, she swallowed a cat!
She swallowed the cat to catch the bird.
How absurd to swallow a bird!
She swallowed the bird to catch the spider
That wiggled and jiggled and tickled inside her.
She swallowed the spider to catch the fly.
I don't know why she swallowed the fly,
Perhaps she'll die.

I know an old lady who swallowed a horse,
She died, of course!

Anon

Lost and Found

I was worrying over some homework
When my grandad walked into the room
And sat wearily down with a grunt and a frown
And a face full of sorrow and gloom.

'I've lost it, I've lost it,' he muttered,
'And it's very important to me.'
'Lost what?' I replied. 'I've forgotten,' he sighed,
'But it's something beginning with T.'

'A toffee, perhaps,' I suggested,
'Or a teapot or even your tie,
Or some toast or a thread . . . ' but he shook his
grey head
As a tear trickled out of one eye.

'A tuba,' I said, 'or some treacle,
Or a toggle to sew on your mac,
Or a tray or a ticket, a tree or a thicket,
A thistle, a taper, a tack.'

But Grandad looked blank. 'Well, some tweezers,
Or a theory,' I said, 'or a tooth,
Or a tap or a till or a thought or a thrill
Or your trousers, a trestle, the truth.'

'It's none of those things,' grumbled Grandad.
'A toy trumpet,' I offered, 'a towel,
Or a trout, a tureen, an antique tambourine,
A toboggan, a tortoise, a trowel . . .'

Then suddenly Grandad's scowl vanished,
'I've remembered!' he cried with a shout.
'It's my temper, you brat, so come here and take
that!'
And he boxed both my ears and stalked out.

Richard Edwards

This is the Ball

This is the ball
That was kicked by the foot
That scored the goal
That won the cup
The day that the final
Was played in our yard.

This is the ball
That flew over the fence
When kicked by the foot
That scored the goal
That won the cup
The day that the final
Was played in our yard.

This is the ball
That flew over the fence
And smashed the window
Of next-door's kitchen
When kicked by the foot
That scored the goal
That won the cup
The day that the final
Was played in our yard.

This is the boy
Who ran away.

This is the boy
Who ran away
To hide in the shed
When he heard the crash
Made by the ball
That flew over the fence
And smashed the window
Of next-door's kitchen

When kicked by the foot
That scored the goal
That won the cup
The day that the final
Was played in our yard.

This is the father
Who found the boy
Who ran away
To hide in the shed
When he heard the crash
Made by the ball
That flew over the fence
And smashed the window
Of next-door's kitchen
When kicked by the foot
That scored the goal
That won the cup
The day that the final
Was played in our yard.

This is the father
Who dragged home the boy
Who ran away
When he heard the crash
Made by the ball
That flew over the fence
And smashed the window
Of next-door's kitchen
When kicked by the foot
That scored the goal
That won the cup
The day that the final
Was played in our yard.

This is the hand
Of the father
Who dragged home the boy
Who ran away
When he heard the crash
Made by the ball
That flew over the fence
And smashed the window
Of next-door's kitchen
When kicked by the foot
That scored the goal
That won the cup
The day that the final
Was played in our yard.

This is the hand
Of the father
Who spanked the boy
Who ran away
When he heard the crash
Made by the ball
That flew over the fence
And smashed the window
Of next-door's kitchen
When kicked by the foot
That scored the goal
That won the cup
The day that the final
Was played in our yard.

And this is the boy
Who can't sit down.

John Foster

What Are Little Boys Made of?

What are little boys made of?
  Frogs and snails
  And puppy-dogs' tails;
That's what little boys are made of.

What are little girls made of?
  Sugar and spice
  And all things nice;
That's what little girls are made of.

Anon

I'd Love to be a Fairy's Child

Children born of fairy stock
Never need for shirt or frock,
Never want for food or fire,
Always get their heart's desire:
Jingle pockets full of gold,
Marry when they're seven years old,
Every fairy child may keep
Two strong ponies and ten sheep;
All have houses, each his own,
Built of brick or granite stone;
They live on cherries, they run wild –
I'd love to be a fairy's child.

Robert Graves

Extremely Naughty Children

By far
The naughtiest
Children
I know
Are Jasper
Geranium
James
And Jo.

They live
In a house
On the Hill
Of Kidd,
And what
In the world
Do you think
They did?

They asked
Their uncles
And aunts
To tea,
And shouted
In loud
Rude voices:
'We
Are tired
of scoldings
And sendings
To bed:
Now
The grown-ups
Shall be
Punished instead.'

They said:
'Auntie Em,
You didn't
Say "Thank You!"
They said:
'Uncle Robert,
We're going
To spank you!'

They pulled
The beard
Of Sir Henry
Dorner
And put him
To stand
In disgrace
In the corner.

They scolded
Aunt B.,
They punished
Aunt Jane;
They slapped
Aunt Louisa
Again
And again.

They said
'Naughty boy!'
To their
Uncle
Fred,
And boxed
His ears
And sent him
To bed.

Do you think
Aunts Em
And Loo
And B.,
And Sir
Henry
Dorner
(K.C.B.),

And the elderly
Uncles
And kind
Aunt Jane
Will go
To tea
With the children
Again?

Elizabeth Godley

If All the World Were Paper

If all the world were paper,
And all the sea were inke;
And all the trees were bread and cheese,
What should we do for drinke?

If all the world were sand 'o,
Oh, then what should we lack 'o;
If as they say there were no clay,
How should we make tobacco?

If all our vessels ran 'a,
If none but had a crack 'a;
If Spanish apes eat all the grapes,
What should we do for sack 'a?

If fryers had no bald pates,
Nor nuns had no dark cloysters,
If all the seas were beans and pease,
What should we do for oysters?

If there had been no projects,
Nor none that did great wrongs;
If fidlers shall turne players all,
What should we doe for songs?

If all things were eternall,
And nothing their end bringing;
If this should be, then, how should we
Here make an end of singing?

Anon

Mice

I think mice
Are rather nice.

Their tails are long,
Their faces small,
They haven't any
Chins at all.
Their ears are pink,
Their teeth are white,
They run about
The house at night.
They nibble things
They shouldn't touch
And no one seems
To like them much.

But I think mice
Are nice.

Rose Fyleman

THE

Growler

Like a toad
beneath a suddenly
flipped stone

huffed up
as if about
to sing (but no

sound comes)
yes, it was me.
I was the one

who cracked the bell
of everyone's *Hey-*
Ring-A-Ding-Ding-

Sweet-Lovers-Love-the . . .
'Stop!' Miss Carver
clapped her hands.

'Which one of you's
the Growler?' No one
breathed. 'Very well.

Sing on.' And she leaned
very close
all down the line till

'Stop!'
She was as small as me
(aged eight)

but sour and sixty,
savage for the love
of her sweet music

I was curdling.
'You!
How *dare* you?

Out!' Down the echoing
hall, all eyes on me . . .
my one big solo.

She died last year.
I hope somebody sang.
Me, I'm still growling.

Philip Gross

Lost in Space

When the space ship first landed
nose down in Dad's prize vegetables
I wasn't expecting the pilot
to be a large blue blob with seven heads
the size and shape of rugby balls
and a toothy grin on his fourteen mouths.

'is this Space Base Six?' he asked
'no' I said 'it's our back garden, number
fifty-two.'
'oh' he said 'are you sure?'
and took from his silver overalls
a shiny book of maps.

There were routes round all the galaxies
ways to the stars through deepest space
maps to planets I'd never heard of
maps to comets, maps to moons
and short cuts to the sun.

'Of course' he said 'silly me,
I turned right, not left, at Venus
easily done, goodbye.'
He shook his heads, climbed inside,
the space ship roared into the sky
and in a shower of leeks and cabbages
disappeared forever.

David Harmer

What Became of Them?

He was a rat, and she was a rat,
  And down in one hole they did dwell,
And both were as black as a witch's cat,
  And they loved one another well.

He had a tail, and she had a tail,
  Both long and curling and fine;
And each said, 'Yours is the finest tail
  In the world, excepting mine.'

He smelt the cheese, and she smelt the cheese,
  And they both pronounced it good;
And both remarked it would greatly add
  To the charms of their daily food.

So he ventured out, and she ventured out,
  And I saw them go with pain;
For what befell them I never can tell,
  For they never came back again.

Anon

The Man in the Wilderness

The man in the wilderness
  Asked me
How many strawberries
  Grew in the sea.

I answered him
  As I thought good,
As many as red herrings
  Grew in the wood.

Anon

The Dragon's Birthday Party

It's the dragon's birthday party,
he's ten years old today.
'Come and do your special trick'
I heard his mother say.

We crowded round the table,
we pushed and shoved to see,
as someone brought the cake mix in
the dragon laughed with glee.

It was just a bowl with flour in
and eggs and milk and that
with ten blue candles round the top
in the shape of Postman Pat.

The dragon took a big deep breath
stood up to his full size
and blew a blast of smoke and flame
that made us shut our eyes.

We felt the air grow hotter
we knew the taste of fear.
I felt a spark fly through the air
and land on my left ear.

But when we looked,
make no mistake:
the candles were lit
and the cake was baked.

Ian McMillan

What You Don't Know About Food

Jelly's made from jellyfish.
Spaghetti's really worms.
Ice cream's just some dirty snow
mixed up with grimy germs.
Bread is made of glue and paste.
So are cakes and pies.
Peanut butter's filled with stuff
like squashed-up lizard eyes.
And as you eat potato chips,
remember all the while –
they're slices of the dried-up brain
of some old crocodile.

Florence Parry Heide

Peas

I eat my peas with honey,
I've done it all my life,
They do taste kind of funny,
But it keeps them on the knife.

Anon

Choosing Their Names

Our old cat has kittens three –
What do you think their names should be?

One is a tabby, with emerald eyes,
  And a tail that's long and slender,
And into a temper she quickly flies
  If you ever by chance offend her:
    I think we shall call her this –
    I think we shall call her that –
Now, don't you think that Pepperpot
  Is a nice name for a cat?

One is black, with a frill of white,
  And her feet are all white fur, too;
If you stroke her she carries her tail upright
  And quickly begins to purr, too!
    I think we shall call her this –
    I think we shall call her that –
Now don't you think that Sootikin
  Is a nice name for a cat?

One is a tortoise-shell, yellow and black,
With plenty of white about him;
If you tease him, at once he sets up his back:
He's a quarrelsome one, ne'er doubt him.
I think we shall call him this –
I think we shall call him that –
Now don't you think that Scratchaway
Is a nice name for a cat?

Our old cat has kittens three
And I fancy their names will be;
Pepperpot, Sootikin, Scratchaway – there!
Were ever kittens with these to compare?
And we call the old mother –
Now, what do you think?
Tabitha Longclaws Tiddley Wink.

Thomas Hood

My Cat is Kind in Winter

My cat is kind in winter
He climbs up on my head
And then he warms my feet at night
By lying on my bed.

Sally Kindberg

There Was an Old Man

There was an Old Man who said, 'Hush!
I perceive a young bird in this bush!'
When they said – 'Is it small?' He replied –
'Not at all!
It is four times as big as the bush!'

Edward Lear

A Swamp Romp

Clomp Thump
Swamp Lump
Plodding in the Ooze,
Belly Shiver
Jelly Quiver
Squelching in my shoes.

Clomp Thump
Romp Jump
Mulching all the Mud,
Boot Trudge
Foot Sludge
Thud! Thud! Thud!

Doug Macleod

Combinations

A flea flew by a bee. The bee
To flee the flea flew by a fly.
The fly flew high to flee the bee
Who flew to flee the flea who flew
To flee the fly who now flew by.

The bee flew by the fly. The fly
To flee the bee flew by the flea.
The flea flew high to flee the fly
Who flew to flee the bee who flew
To flee the flea who now flew by.

The fly flew by the flea. The flea
To flee the fly flew by the bee.
The bee flew high to flee the flea
Who flew to flee the fly who flew
To flee the bee who now flew by.

The flea flew by the fly. The fly
To flee the flea flew by the bee.
The bee flew high to flee the fly
Who flew to flee the flea who flew
To flee the bee who now flew by.

The fly flew by the bee. The bee
To flee the fly flew by the flea.
The flea flew high to flee the bee
Who flew to flee the fly who flew
To flee the flea who now flew by.

The bee flew by the flea. The flea
To flee the bee flew by the fly.
The fly flew high to flee the flea
Who flew to flee the bee who flew
To flee the fly who now flew by.

Mary Ann Hoberman

Mr Nobody

I know a funny little man,
As quiet as a mouse.
He does the mischief that is done
In everybody's house.
Though no one ever sees his face,
Yet one and all agree
That every plate we break, was cracked
By Mr Nobody.

'Tis he who always tears our books,
Who leaves the door ajar.
He picks the buttons from our shirts,
And scatters pins afar.
That squeaking door will always squeak –
For prithee, don't you see?
We leave the oiling to be done
By Mr Nobody.

He puts damp wood upon the fire,
That kettles will not boil:
His are the feet that bring in mud
And all the carpets soil.
The papers that so oft are lost –
Who had them last but he?
There's no one tosses them about
But Mr Nobody.

The fingermarks upon the door
By none of us were made.
We never leave the blinds unclosed
To let the curtains fade.
The ink we never spill! The boots
That lying round you see,
Are not our boots – they all belong
To Mr Nobody.

Anon

The Donkey

I saw a donkey
One day old,
His head was too big
For his neck to hold;
His legs were shaky
And long and loose,
They rocked and staggered
And weren't much use.

He tried to gambol
And frisk a bit,
But he wasn't quite sure
Of the trick of it.
His queer little coat
Was soft and grey,
And curled at his neck
In a lovely way.
His face was wistful
And left no doubt
That he felt life needed
Some thinking about.
So he blundered around
In venturesome quest,
And then lay flat
On the ground to rest.

He looked so little
And weak and slim,
I prayed the world
Might be good to him.

Anon

See a Penny

See a penny
Pick it up
All the day you'll have good luck.

One hundred pennies
Make a pound;
One hundred days:
Keep your eyes on the ground!

Three months,
One week,
And a day or two –
Then you'll find your lucky pound
Saved up for you.

Dave Ward

Water Everywhere

There's water on the ceiling,
And water on the wall,
There's water in the bedroom,
And water in the hall,
There's water on the landing,
And water on the stair,
Whenever Daddy takes a bath
There's water everywhere.

Valerie Bloom

James Had a Magic Set for Christmas

James had practised the tricks for days
but in front of the class
they all went wrong.
The invisible penny
dropped from his sleeve,
the secret pocket
failed to open,
his magic wand broke.
'Perhaps another time,' Miss Burroughs
suggested,
'another day
when you've the hang of it.'

'No, Miss! Please!
I can do them, honestly.'

Suddenly
a white rabbit was sitting
on Miss Burroughs' table,
a green snake, tongue flicking,
scattered the class from the carpet,
the school was showered with golden coins
that rolled into piles on the playground.
'But, James!' Miss Burroughs said. 'Shouldn't –'

There was a flash of lightning.
While the fire brigade coaxed
Miss Burroughs down from the oak
she'd flown into
on the other side of the playground,
the caretaker quietly swept up the mess
and Mr Pinner, the headmaster,
confiscated the magic set.
'A rather dangerous toy,' he said, 'James!'

James is still asking for it back.

Brian Morse

I Had a Little Nut Tree

I had a little nut tree,
Nothing would it bear,
But a silver nutmeg,
And a golden pear.
The King of Spain's daughter
Came to visit me,
And all was because of
My little nut tree.
I skipped over water
I danced over sea,
And all the birds in the air
Could not catch me.

Anon

A Night I Had Trouble Falling Asleep

I stayed over at Eliot's house.
'I've lost my pet,' he said.
'So please wake me up in the middle of the night
If you find a big snake in your bed.'

Jeff Moss

Mary, Mary Quite Contrary

Mary has a little lamb
But she'd rather have a gerbil
She'd dress it up in Barbie's clothes
And paint its toenails purple.

Lindsay MacRae

The Cabbage is a Funny Veg

The cabbage is a funny veg.
All crisp, and green, and brainy.
I sometimes wear one on my head
When it's cold and rainy.

Roger McGough

Aliens Stole My Underpants

To understand the ways
of alien beings is hard,
and I've never worked it out
why they landed in my backyard.

And I've always wondered why
on their journey from the stars,
these aliens stole my underpants
and took them back to Mars.

They came on a Monday night
when the weekend wash had been done,
pegged out on the line
to be dried by the morning sun.

Mrs Driver from next door
was a witness at the scene
when aliens snatched my underpants –
I'm glad that they were clean!

It seems they were quite choosy
as nothing else was taken.
Do aliens wear underpants
or were they just mistaken?

I think I have a theory
as to what they wanted them for,
they needed to block off a draught
blowing in through the spacecraft door.

Or maybe some Mars museum
wanted items brought back from Space
Just think, my pair of Y-fronts
displayed in their own glass case.

And on the label beneath
would be written where they got 'em
and how such funny underwear
once covered an Earthling's bottom!

Brian Moses

Orange End

'Oh fantasy of great oranges in the trees
Will you let me eat you in extraordinary silence'

'Oh yes my life has ended
Oh gentle maiden pick me and eat me –
Ouch!'

Laura Newhofer (7)

Pass the Pasta!

Spud
is good,
rice
is nice,
but pasta
is faster!

Judith Nicholls

My Cousin Melda

My Cousin Melda
she don't make fun
she ain't afraid of anyone
even mosquitoes
when they bite her
she does bite them back
and say –
'Now tell me, how you like that?'

Grace Nichols

Daddy Fell into the Pond

Everyone grumbled. The sky was grey.
We had nothing to do and nothing to say.
We were nearing the end of a dismal day.
And there seemed to be nothing beyond,
  Then
    Daddy fell into the pond!

And everyone's face grew merry and bright,
And Timothy danced for sheer delight.
'Give me the camera, quick, oh quick!
He's crawling out of the duckweed!' Click!

Then the gardener suddenly slapped his knee,
And doubled up, shaking silently,
And the ducks all quacked as if they were daft,
And it sounded as if the old drake laughed.
Oh, there wasn't a thing that didn't respond
  When
    Daddy fell into the pond!

Alfred Noyes

St Jerome and His Lion

St Jerome in his study kept a great big cat,
It's always in his pictures, with its feet upon the
  mat.
Did he give it milk to drink, in a little dish?
When it came to Fridays, did he give it fish?
If I lost my little cat, I'd be sad without it;
I should ask St Jeremy what to do about it;
I should ask St Jeremy, just because of that,
For he's the only saint I know who kept a
  pussy cat.

Anon

My Dragon

My pet dragon lived in my pencil pot.
She was as small as a tennis ball.
She threw my pencils out.
When I told my friends,
they said I was a liar.
I said, 'Only because
you haven't got one!'
My mum thought my dragon
was my teddy Gizmo.
When my dragon got bigger,
her eyes were pieces
of melted red glass.
She cooked my dinner
with her breath. I shared
my egg and chips with her.
She drank acid bombs.

My dragon is dead now.
I buried her in the garden
under the shed with Gizmo.

Steven Barnett (7)

Asking Questions

When I ask my Mum: 'What's for tea?'
She smiles and says, 'Wait and see!'

When I ask my Dad what things he's done,
He smiles and says, 'In a minute, son.'

When I ask my Gran if I can watch TV
'I'll think about it,' she says to me.

When I ask my Gramps about the good old days,
'Now you're asking,' he smiles and says.

If I answer the questions my teacher asks me
With 'In a minute' or 'Wait and see,'
I know just what the result would be!

Gervase Phinn

Jealousy

Jealousy is dark blue.
Jealousy is when Samuel
is getting a cuddle
And I'm
on the settee without one.
Jealousy sounds like crying and huffiness.
Jealousy tastes sour in your throat.
Jealousy smells like sweat and sort of strange.
Jealousy feels like you have two hearts,
One going up in anger,
And one going down with sadness.

Stephanie Reynolds (7)

Girl From a Train

We stopped by a cornfield
Near Shrewsbury
A girl in a sun hat
Smiled at me.

Then I was seven
Now sixty-two
Wherever you are
I remember you.

Gareth Owen

Squeezes

We love to squeeze bananas
We love to squeeze ripe plums
And when we're feeling sad
We love to squeeze our mums.

Brian Patten

Fishy!

At the Sea Life Centre
There were plenty of fish,
Floating and gliding or
Chasing about,
But although we saw
Fish tails and fish scales,
Teeth and mouths,
Whiskers and fins,
We didn't see any
Fishfingers!

Brian Moses

What is Pink?

What is pink? A rose is pink
By the fountain's brink.
What is red? A poppy's red
In its barley bed.
What is blue? The sky is blue
Where the clouds float through.
What is white? A swan is white
Sailing in the light.
What is yellow? Pears are yellow,
Rich and ripe and mellow.
What is green? The grass is green,
With small flowers between.
What is violet? Clouds are violet
In the summer twilight.
What is orange? Why, an orange,
Just an orange!

Christina Rossetti

Have You Ever Done Any Cooking?

Have you ever done any cooking? Here's me talking to my Mum after I've been doing some cooking.

You know you said I could do some cooking
and you know you said you wouldn't be looking

'cos I wanted to give you a nice surprise
and make a few cakes, make a few pies,

but you said, OK. You did say, 'Yes.'
Well, I'm really sorry, but there's a bit of a mess.

I mean to say, in about an hour,
you can use quite a lot of flour.

So don't get angry when you come in the door
but most of the flour is on the floor.

The rolling pin seems to be covered in dirt
and milk has soaked right through my shirt.

A bit of butter has stuck to the chair
though most of it seems to be in my hair.

Yes, I can guess just what you think.
And the raisins. I forgot. They're in the sink.

So I'm really sorry, but I didn't finish the cakes.
Like you say. We all make mistakes.

Michael Rosen

Pony Trap Rap

I've ridden in,
And on, most things
That you can think of:
Things with wings
And things with wheels,
Things with rudders,
Things with keels;
Buses, barges,
Tandems, trikes,
Scooters, skiffs
And motor bikes;
Rickshaws, sledges,
Skates and skis,
Vauxhall Vivas,
Ford Capris;
Helicopters,
Submarines,
Balloons and zeppelins,
Flying-machines;
Speed boats, schooners,
Once on a raft;
Canoes and ferry-boats,
Hovercraft.

I've ridden solo,
Pillion too;
I've soared so high,
Right out of view;
Sailed as a passenger
And as crew.
But there's one thing
That I must do
That I have never
Done before,
Something simple
I'd adore:
I long to drive
A pony and trap,
And hear the delicate
Tippety-tap
Of the pony's hooves
Down country lanes,
And sit up proud
And hold the reins,
And wear a billycock
Or flat cap;
I'd look a proper
Country chap.
I'd dump my compass
Rip up map,

And stay at home
Not care a scrap
As long as I had
My pony and trap;
As long as I had
My
  pony
    and
        trap.

Vernon Scannell

Who Has Seen the Wind?

Who has seen the wind?
Neither I nor you:
But when the leaves hang trembling
The wind is passing through.

Who has seen the wind?
Neither you nor I:
But when the trees bow down their heads
The wind is passing by.

Christina Rossetti

Squatter's Rights

Listen, kitten,
Get this clear;
This is my chair,
I sit here.

OK, kitty,
We can share;
When I'm not home,
It's your chair.

Listen, tom cat,
How about
If I use it
When you're out?

Richard Shaw

O Dandelion

'O dandelion, yellow as gold,
What do you do all day?'

'I just wait here in the tall green grass
Till the children come to play.'

'O dandelion, yellow as gold,
What do you do all night?'

'I wait and wait till the cool dews fall
And my hair grows long and white.'

'And what do you do when your hair is white
And the children come to play?'

'They take me up in their dimpled hands
And blow my hair away!'

Anon

The Football Family Man

I'm the finest fan
that football's had.
I've a football gran
with a football fad.
I've a football mother
and a football dad.
And my football brother
has football bad.

With my football wife
in our football pad
to our football life
we football add
two football daughters
and a football lad,
all football supporters,
all football mad.

We've football dogs.
They're football clad
in football togs
like a football ad.
For our football ways,
we're football glad.
Without football days
we'd be football sad.

I'm a football man
who's football mad.
I'm the finest fan
that football's had.
I'm the football family man.

Nick Toczek

The Star

Twinkle, twinkle, little star,
How I wonder what you are!
Up above the world so high,
Like a diamond in the sky.

When the blazing sun is gone,
When he nothing shines upon,
Then you show your little light,
Twinkle, twinkle, all the night.

Then the traveller in the dark,
Thanks you for your tiny spark,
He could not see which way to go,
If you did not twinkle so.

In the dark blue sky you keep,
And often through my curtains peep,
For you never shut your eye,
Till the sun is in the sky.

As your bright and tiny spark,
Lights the traveller in the dark –
Though I know not what you are,
Twinkle, twinkle, little star.

Jane Tayler

Blubberbelly Wobblewalk Stumblebum Smith

When I was young, I made friends with
Blubberbelly Wobblewalk Stumblebum Smith,
a proper live dragon, not just a myth.

Lonely and large as a monolith,
Blubberbelly Wobblewalk Stumblebum Smith
had no parents, kin or kith.

One day I was cruel. He left forthwith,
Blubberbelly Wobblewalk Stumblebum Smith,
for a secret place he called his frith.

I often wish I'd made up with
Blubberbelly Wobblewalk Stumblebum Smith,
who never returned after our daft tiff.

Was he real or merely a myth?
Blubberbelly Wobblewalk Stumblebum Smith,
the dragon I used to be friends with.

Nick Toczek

Windy Nights

Whenever the moon and stars are set,
  Whenever the wind is high,
All night long in the dark and wet,
  A man goes riding by.
Late in the night when the fires are out,
  Why does he gallop and gallop about?

Whenever the trees are crying aloud,
  And ships are tossed at sea,
By, on the highway, low and loud,
  By at the gallop goes he.
By at the gallop he goes, and then
  By he comes back at the gallop again.

R.L. Stevenson

Night Fun

I hear eating.
I hear drinking.
I hear music.
I hear laughter.
Fun is something
Grown-ups never have
Before my bedtime.
Only after.

Judith Viorst

Starlight

Starlight,
Starbright.
First star I see tonight,
I wish I may,
I wish I might,
Have this wish I wish tonight.

Anon

Ten–Nil

The phantom fans are chanting
There's a cheer in my ear as I score:
I've done it again: ten goals to me
And nil to the garage door!

Celia Warren

Snowdrops

I like to think
  That, long ago,
There fell to earth
  Some flakes of snow
Which loved this cold,
  Grey world of ours
So much, they stayed
  As snowdrop flowers.

Mary Vivian

New Shoes

My shoes are new and squeaky shoes,
They're shiny, creaky shoes,
I wish I had my leaky shoes
That my mother threw away.

I liked my old brown leaky shoes
Much better than these creaky shoes,
These shiny, creaky, squeaky shoes
I've got to wear today.

Anon

The Dark Wood

In the dark, dark wood, there was
    a dark, dark house,
And in that dark, dark house, there was
    a dark, dark room,
And in that dark, dark room, there was
    a dark, dark cupboard,
And in that dark, dark cupboard, there was
    a dark, dark shelf,
And on that dark, dark shelf, there was
    a dark, dark box,
And in that dark, dark box, there was a

GHOST!

Anon

Acknowledgements

The compiler and publishers wish to thank the following for permission to use copyright material:

John Agard, 'Mother Alligator's Advice To Her Children' from *I Din Do Nuttin and Other Poems*, Bodley Head, by permission of Random House UK; and 'No Hickory No Dickory No Dock' from *No Hickory No Dickory No Dock*, Viking (1991), by permission of Caroline Sheldon Literary Agency on behalf of the author; **Allan Ahlberg**, 'Bedtime' from *Please Mrs Butler* by Allan Ahlberg, Kestrel. Copyright © Allan Ahlberg 1983, by permission of Penguin Books; **Steven Barnett**, 'My Dragon' from *Electric Full Stops* (1995) Young Writers Competition, by permission of W H Smith; **Valerie Bloom**, 'Water Everywhere', by permission of the author; **Charles Causley**, ' "Quack" Said the Billy-Goat' from *Collected Poems for Children* by Charles Causley, Macmillan, by permission of David Higham Associates on behalf of the author; **Andrew Collett**, 'Christmas Eve Trip', by permission of the author; **Paul Cookson**, 'Barry and Beryl the Bubble Gum Blowers', first published in *The Toilet Seat Has Teeth!*, A Twist in the Tale (1992) and 'Mum for a Day', first published in *The Amazing Captain Corcorde, A Twist in the Tale* (1990), by permission of the author; **Wendy Cope**, 'Twiddling Your Thumbs' from *Twiddling Your Thumbs*, Faber (1988), by permission of Peters Fraser & Dunlop Group Ltd on behalf of the author; **Peter Dixon**, 'Magic Cat' and 'Muuuuuuummmmmmm' from *Grand Prix* by Peter Dixon, Macmillan, by permission of the author; **Richard Edwards**, 'Bramble Talk' and 'Lost and Found' from *A Mouse in My Roof*, (1988), by permission of the author; **John Foster**, 'This Is the Ball' an extract from 'Football Story', first published in *Four O'Clock Friday*, Oxford University Press. Copyright © 1991 John Foster, by permission of the author; **Rose Fyleman**, 'Mice', by permission of The Society of Authors as the literary representative of the Estate of the author; **Robert Graves**, 'I'd Love to Be a Fairy's Child' from *Complete Poems*, by permission of Carcanet Press Ltd; **David Harmer**, 'Lost in Space, by permission of the author; **Mary Ann Hoberman**, 'Combinations' from *The Llama Who Had No Pajamas*, Browndeer Press/Harcourt Brace. Copyright © 1976, 1998 by Mary Ann Hoberman, by permission of Gina Maccoby Literary Agency on behalf of the author; **Lindsay MacRae**, 'Mary, Mary Quite Contrary' from *You Canny Shove Yer Granny off a Bus!*, Viking. Copyright © Lindsay MacRae, 1995, by permission of The Agency (London) Ltd on behalf of the author; **Ian McMillan**, 'The Dragon's Birthday Party', by permission of the author; **Roger McGough**, 'The Cabbage Is a Funny Veg' from *Sky in the Pie*, Kestrel (1983), by permission of of Peters Fraser & Dunlop Group Ltd on behalf of the author; **Eve Merriam**, 'Peculiar' from *Jamboree Rhymes for All Times* by Eve Merriam. Copyright © 1962, 1964, 1973, 1984 by Eve Merriam, by permission of Marian Reiner on behalf of the Estate of the author; **Trevor**

Millum, 'Dick's Dog', Macmillan by permission of the author; **Brian Morse**, 'James Had a Magic Set for Christmas' from *Picnic on the Moon*, by permission of Turton & Chambers Ltd; **Brian Moses**, 'Aliens Stole My Underpants' from *Don't Look at Me in that Tone of Voice*, Macmillan, and 'Fishy!' from *An Odd Kettle of Fish*, Macmillan, by permission of the author; **Jeff Moss**, 'A Night I Had Trouble Falling Asleep' from *The Butterfly Jar*, by permission of ICM, Inc on behalf of the author; **Laura Newhofer**, 'Orange End' from *Young Words* (1989), Young Writers Competition, by permission of W H Smith; **Grace Nichols**, 'My Cousin Melda' from *Come On Into My Tropical Garden*, A & C Black. Copyright © 1994 by Grace Nichols, by permission of Curtis Brown Ltd, London, on behalf of the author; **Alfred Noyes**, 'Daddy Fell into the Pond' from *Collected Poems*, by permission of John Murray (Publishers) Ltd; **David Orme**, 'Town Dog', by permission of the author; **Gareth Owen**, 'Girl From a Train', first published in *The Fox on the Roundabout*, Collins Young Lions (1995), by permission Rogers, Coleridge & White Ltd on behalf of the author; **Gervase Phinn**, 'Asking Questions' from *Classroom Creatures* (1996), by permission of the author; **Stephanie Reynolds**, 'Jealousy' from *Electric Full Stops* (1995), Young Writers Competition, by permission of W H Smith; **Michael Rosen**, 'Have You Ever Done Any Cooking?' from *Never Mind!*, BBC/Longman (1990), by permission of Peters Fraser & Dunlop Group Ltd on behalf of the author; **Vernon Scannell**, 'Pony Trap Rap', by permission of the author; **Nick Toczek**, 'Blubberbelly Wobblewlk Sumblebum Smith' from *Dragons Everywhere* by Nick Toczek, Macmillan (1998) and 'The Football Family Man' from *They Think It's All Over*, ed. David Orme, Macmillan (1995), by permission of the author; **Judith Viorst**, 'Night Fun' from *If I Were in Charge of the World and Other Worries* (1981). Copyright © Judith Viorst 1981, by permission of A M Heath on behalf of the author and Scholastic Australia Pty Ltd; **Dave Ward**, 'See a Penny' from *Candy and Jazz* by Dave Ward, Oxford University Press (1994), by permission of the author; **Celia Warren**, 'Ten-Nil', by permission of the author; Every effort has been made to trace the copyright holders but if any have been inadvertently overlooked the publishers will be pleased to make the necessary arrangement at the first opportunity.